The Wrong Wheels

by

C. L. Tompsett

Illustrated by Julia Page

First published in 2008 in Great Britain by
Barrington Stoke Ltd
18 Walker St, Edinburgh, EH3 7LP

www.barringtonstoke.co.uk

Title ISBN: 978-1-84299-635-5
Pack ISBN: 978-1-84299-623-2

Printed in Poland by Pozkal

We ask the author ...

If you could buy any car, what would it be?

If I could buy any car, I would buy a red Ferrari because it is fast, it looks good and it would make me feel cool.

Troy came to school in his new white trainers.

His teacher told him that he must wear black shoes in school.

Troy didn't care because he liked his new trainers.

"Do you like my trainers?" Troy asked Greg and Sam.

Greg and Sam nodded.

They both wanted trainers like Troy's.

Greg had asked his mum for some trainers last night but she had said, "No. They cost too much."

At break, Greg went outside with Sam. They kicked a ball around.

Sam was hungry so he ate a ham sandwich.

Troy grinned at Sam. "Call that a sandwich? This is more like it!"

He was eating a big sandwich with egg, bacon and tomato.

"Have it if you want," he said and chucked it at Sam.

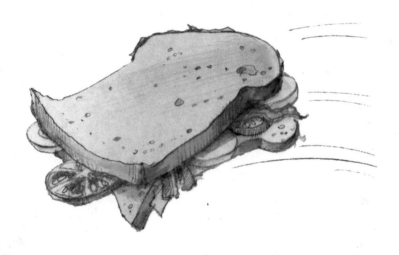

The bell went for the end of break and Greg and Sam went back into class.

Troy came in late.

"I don't like him," Greg said to Sam. "He thinks he's IT because he is so rich."

"I wish I was as rich as him," Sam said.

At half past three, school ended and Troy went home.

His mum was in the kitchen.

"Dad's home," she said. "He's got a surprise for you."

"What's that?" Troy asked.

He hoped Dad had got him the new
Playstation game he'd asked for.

Dad was in the living room.

He was smiling.

"I've passed my driving test at last," he said to Troy. "And I'm going to buy a car."

"Great!" Troy said. "You can take me out in it. What make of car is it?"

Dad smiled again.

"Do you know 'Pete's Cars' at the end of Park Road?" he asked.

"Yes," said Troy. "I pass it on the way to school."

"Well, I'm going to buy the blue car that's parked at the front," Dad told him.

Troy had looked at that car every day on the way home from school. It was his dream car.

It was a Subaru.

And now his dad was going to buy it!

"Go on, tell him the rest," Mum said. She shook Dad's arm.

"Well, your mum and I have agreed that you can have it next year. You will be 17 then and I'll buy myself another car."

Troy didn't sleep at all that night. He just had to have that car.

The next day, he stopped at 'Pete's Cars' on his way to school.

The Subaru was there at the front.

The blue body work was shining.

The gold alloy wheels were shining.

"Soon that will be mine!" Troy said to himself.

He ran off to school to tell everyone.

Greg and Sam walked into school.

They saw a lot of boys around Troy.

"What's going on?" Greg asked one of the boys.

"Troy's dad has got him a car!" one of the boys said. "A Subaru."

"Yeah, right," Greg said. "Maybe a toy one in a box."

Troy came up to Greg and Sam.

"No, it is a real one," he said. "It's blue with gold alloy wheels. It can do 140 miles an hour easy. Dad's got it for himself, but he says I can have it when I'm 17."

Troy suddenly found he had a lot of friends. They all wanted to see his car.

"I still don't like him," Greg said to Sam.

"He's just a big show-off."

"Yes I know," Sam said.

"But he's a show-off with a nice car."

Sam walked off to join Troy.

"Where is your Subaru, then?" Greg yelled after Troy. "I don't think your Dad has got one at all."

"He's picking it up soon," Troy yelled back.

"Then I'll get him to bring me to school in it. And you'll see!"

Troy was in a hurry to get home from school. He wanted to know when his dad was picking up the car.

"When are you getting our new car?" he asked his dad.

"It's not a new car," his dad told him. "You've seen it. It's the blue one at 'Pete's Cars'."

"I know it's not new," Troy said. "But it's still a great car! When are we getting it?"

Troy's dad grinned at him. "We? It's my car until next year, you know!"

"But then it will be mine! Won't it, Dad?" Troy said.

Troy's dad smiled. "If you still want it."

Troy's eyes opened wide.

"You bet I'll want it! Everyone wants one."

"Well, let's go then. I'm going to pick it up now."

Troy ran all the way to 'Pete's Cars'.

Then he had to wait for his dad, because his dad was not as fast as him.

Troy waited by the blue Subaru.

"There you are, son," his dad said. "Nice car, isn't it?"

But Troy's dad walked on past the Subaru.

"This is our car," he said.

He pointed to a blue Ford Escort.

"But you said ..." said Troy.

Troy's dad looked back at the Subaru.

"Oh no," he said. "That's too fast for me.
I've only just passed my test. Get in and I'll
drive us home. I'll even drive you to school
tomorrow."

Troy had been a show-off.

He'd told his friends what a super car he was getting. They would take the mick out of him when they saw him in the blue Ford Escort.

"No thanks, Dad," he said. "I think I'll walk."